PRETTY PERFECT KITTY-CORN

To Sam, our newest itty-bitty kitty baby
—S.H. & L.P.

ISBN 978-1-339-03536-9

12 11 10 9 8 7 6 5 4 3 2 1   23 24 25 26 27 28

Printed in the U.S.A.   40

This edition first printing, September 2023

Book design by Pamela Notarantonio
The illustrations for this book were created entirely in Procreate.

PRETTY PERFECT KITTY-CORN

SHANNON HALE & LEUYEN PHAM

SCHOLASTIC INC.

UNiCORN is perfect.
Everybody thinks so.

"His horn is shiny; his coat is clean," says Gecko.

"His tail is as purple as a dream," says Parakeet.

Even his best **Kitty-CORN** friend thinks so.

"You're perfect!" says **Kitty**.

"Stay right there. I'm going to paint you."

UNICORN holds as still as a marble statue. He yearns to look the way everyone thinks he should.

"He is simply resplendent from hooves to horn," says Parakeet.

"There's no one more perfect than Unicorn," says Gecko.

"Hmm, something is missing
from my painting," says **Kitty**.
"It just doesn't look right."

Not right? Is **UNiCORN** doing something wrong?

He lowers his magnificent haunches.

He stretches his neck long.

He reclines majestically.

Perhaps now he looks perfect.

"He's so flawless and so faultless that he's frankly sublime!" says Parakeet.

"My affection for his perfection makes it easy to rhyme," says Gecko.

"Something is still missing!"
says **Kitty**.

Oh no! **UNiCORN** stands and twists,
sways and spins, gallops in place, and
poses thoughtfully—all at the same time.

"That's it! It's perfect!"
exclaims **Kitty**.

Kitty adds a final mark to her canvas.

"Come and behold my masterpiece!"

Gecko gapes. "What
do I see?"
Parakeet gawks. "No,
it can't be . . ."

But it is. **UNICORN** must
have sat in some paint.
UNICORN has a . . .

"His mane is purple; his horn is shiny," says Gecko.

"But there's paint all over his huge white heinie!" says Parakeet.

"UNiCORN?" asks Kitty.

"Are you OK?"

UNiCORN is not OK. Even the potted plant can't hide his shame. He feels like a big, ugly goof.

"Just ignore Gecko and Parakeet," says **Kitty**.

"I don't care that they saw me with a paint bum," says **UNiCORN**.

"Then why are you sad?"

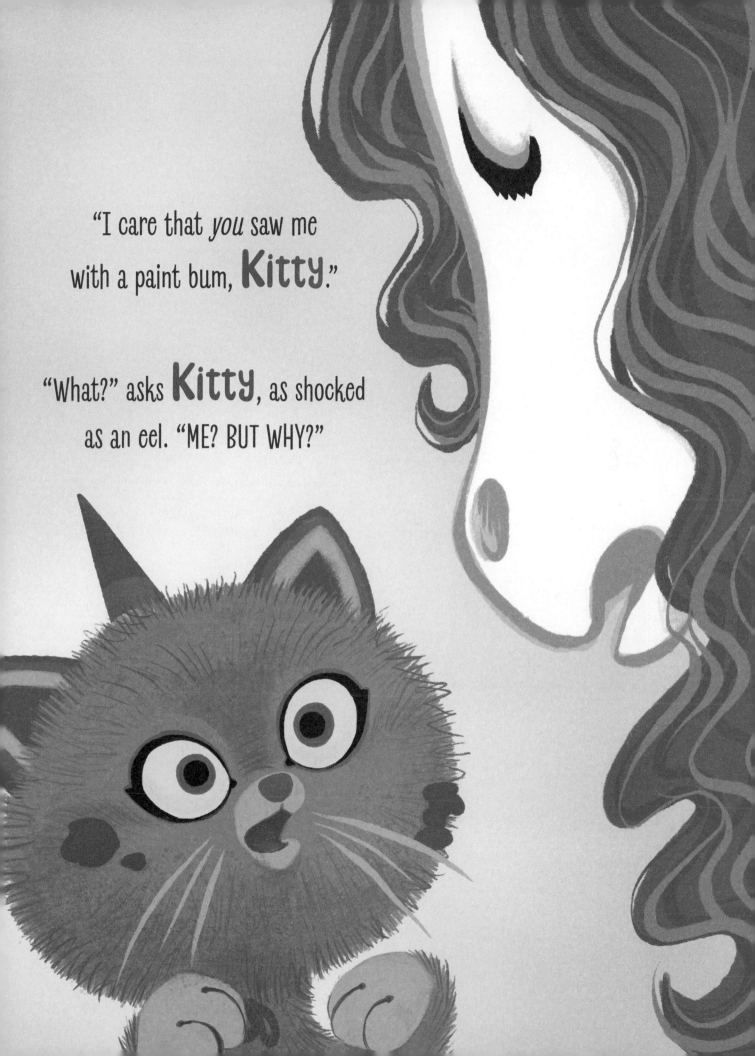

"I care that *you* saw me
with a paint bum, **Kitty**."

"What?" asks **Kitty**, as shocked
as an eel. "ME? BUT WHY?"

UNiCORN doesn't know how to say it. How **Kitty** is the twin of his heart. How she is precious, like the last cookie.

And how he worries that, unless he's perfect, **Kitty** might not want to be his friend anymore.

But all he can say is "Because I just like you so much."

Kitty says, "I just like you so much too."

UNICORN is messy.

He has paint on his horn and the tips of his kitten ears. He has paint on his gold hooves and the ends of his tail. And he has a huge, glorious paint bum.

He'll definitely have a bath later.
Warm and long, with plenty of
bubbles to wash away the goop.

But for now, with **Kitty**,
he can be messy.

With his best **Kitty-CORN** friend, **UNICORN** can be anything.

LeUyen Pham and **Shannon Hale** are the team behind the bestselling picture book *Itty-Bitty Kitty-Corn*, the bestselling graphic novels *Real Friends, Best Friends,* and *Friends Forever,* and with Dean Hale, the early chapter book series The Princess in Black. They've made a bunch of other books too. They are both: moms of kids who aren't afraid to get messy, wives to husbands who make art, honor award winners (Caldecott and Newbery), caretakers of cats, and believers in unicorns. LeUyen lives in Los Angeles, Shannon lives in Utah, and with each other, they know they can be—and make—anything.